The Garden In My Heart

A book about sowing and reaping

Written and illustrated by Nikki Rogers

When a farmer wants
a tomato plant to grow,
the farmer knows exactly
the seed he needs to sow.
The farmer takes the seed
and puts it in good ground,
covers it with soil
and waters all around.

Sometimes it takes a while
before he sees the fruit,
but he continues to care for that seed
and believes its taking root.
Although it may just look like dirt
even for quite a while,
when seedlings shoot up from the
ground the farmer's sure to smile.

There is a secret garden
inside every girl and boy
and there are special seeds to plant
that will grow into joy.

If you want your garden to be filled
with life and happy days,
plant lots of seeds of thankfulness
and sing out songs of praise.
Sow the seeds of patience
instead of getting mad.
Take the time to think about
the things that make you glad.

If you want friends, sow friendship
into one another.
Water those seeds with love
and show kindness to each other.
Sow seeds of compassion
and water them generously.
Appreciate the things you have
and beauty you will see.

Some people come and sow things like
bitterness or greed
that grow into an ugly plant
you don't want called a weed.
If you see a weed like jealousy
sprout in your garden bed,
pull it out immediately
and sow thankfulness instead.

When you sow seeds of goodness
it's not only good for you,
but your plants can bring joy
to other people too!
Some people might find shelter under
your comfort tree,
or they might smell the sweetness
from the flowers that they see.

You can share from your garden
the fruit the people need
and inside every piece of fruit
hides another precious seed.
If they take those seeds inside
and in their hearts they sow
and water it and care for it
that plant is sure to grow.

Everyone wants good fruit to eat
and lovely gardens to own,
but every plant you see is from
a seed that has been sown.
If you want your garden beautiful
then handle it with care.
Make sure you only sow the seeds
for plants you want in there!

Each person has a garden
deep within their heart
and whatever seed is sown there
a plant is sure to start.
So remember to plant good seeds and
water them everyday
and if you see a weed spring up
pull it out straight away!

Written with love for my husband, Simon, who demonstrates what a life full of good fruit looks like.

More inspirational Children's Books by Nikki Rogers

* A Beautiful Girl

* A Hero Is

For more info visit www.createdtobe.com.au

All books are also available as eBooks

Like us at www.facebook.com/created.to.be.you

About the Author

I am a mother of two, a little girl and a little boy. I originally started writing children's stories with values that I wanted to instill in my own children when, with encouragement, I realized I wanted these inspiring values shared with parents and children all over the world.

All my children's books are written with this in mind: that I would inspire children and parents to be all they were created to be.

I also have a desire to see people, especially children, all over the world set free from whatever holds them bound and so all the profit from my books goes toward various world missions that fight for this cause.

Made in the USA
San Bernardino, CA
13 June 2014